We Like To Help Cook

We Like to Help Cook

MARCUS ALLSOP

Illustrations by Diane Iverson

HOHM PRESS
Prescott, Arizona

Cover design: Zachary Parker
Book layout and design: Zachary Parker, Kadak Graphics, Prescott, Arizona

Library of Congress Cataloging in Publication Data:

Allsop, Marcus.
  We like to help cook / Marcus Allsop ; illustrations by Diane Iverson.
     p. cm.
  ISBN 1-890772-70-4 (pbk. : alk. paper)
  1. Nutrition--Juvenile literature. 2. Food--Juvenile literature. I. Iverson, Diane, ill. II. Title.
  RA784.A446 2007
  613.2083--dc22
                        2006036359

HOHM PRESS
P.O. Box 2501
Prescott, AZ 86302
800-381-2700
http://www.hohmpress.com

This book was printed in China.

Cover Illustration: Diane Iverson, www.dianeiverson.com

Thanks to Lee and the entire Hohm Press team.

We like to help cook, all kinds of foods—
good for our bodies and good for our moods.

We wash our hands and find a place—
one that is stable and one that is safe.
With a grown-up in charge, we can do... or just look...
We like to help, we like to cook.

We can help by washing foods ...
like brown rice or white.
Running the grains under water,
we watch until the water runs clear.

We like to measure things ...
whole-grain pasta for the pot.
We can try all shapes and sizes:
bowties, noodles or spirals.

We know how to mash ...
avocados with tomatoes.
When the lumps are all smooth, we have a dip
for our celery, carrot sticks or tortilla chips.

We like to tear up ...
lettuce or other leafy greens.
Lots of different colors make our salad like a rainbow—
purple cabbage, yellow corn and bright orange carrots.

We like to mix ...
oatmeal with water or milk.
Sometimes we add in other favorite foods,
like raisins or nuts.

We like to place things ...
like slices of fruit, to make a face on our plate.
We can use apples, blueberries, bananas,
grapes and pears.

We like to toss ...
fresh salad vegetables with healthy oils
like sunflower or olive oil.
It's fun to use big spoons or tongs.

We like to shake up or blend ...
With lowfat milk or yogurt we can help make
a smoothie or milkshake.

We like to crumble ...
low-fat cheese on many foods,
like baked potatoes, wholegrain crackers
or noodles.

We like to rinse ...
dried peas and beans, which are full of proteins.
We have so many choices —
black-eyed peas, pintos, garbanzo beans ...

We like to watch ...
while grown-ups cook,
grilling extra-lean meat, fish or skinless chicken.
Sometimes we can guess what is cooking
just from the sounds and smells.

We like to work ... help cook ... and play.
We like being active every day.

OTHER FAMILY-HEALTH / WORLD-HEALTH TITLES FROM HOHM PRESS:

We Like To Nurse Too
by M. Young
Design by Zachary Parker
Captivating and colorful illustrations present mother sea-animals nursing their young. The warmly encouraging and simple text supports the relationship of nursing.
ISBN: 978-1-890772-98-7, paper, 32 pages, $9.95
Bi-lingual Version: *También a Nosotros Nos Gusta Amamantar*
ISBN: 978-1-890772-99-4

We Like Our Teeth
Written and Illustrated by Marcus Allsop
A picture book for children and parents that encourages kids to care for their teeth with bright, whimsical images of animals caring for their own teeth.
ISBN: 978-1-890772-86-4, paper, 32 pages, $9.95
Bilingual Version: *Nos Gustan Nuestros Dientes*
ISBN: 978-1-890772-89-5

We Like To Play Music
by Kate Parker
Design by Zachary Parker
An easy-to-read picture book with photos of children playing music, moving to a beat and enjoying music alone and with parents and peers.
ISBN: 978-1-890772-85-7, paper, 32 pages, $9.95
Bi-lingual Version: *Nos Gusta Tocar Música*
ISBN: 978-1-890772-90-1

We Like To Eat Well
by Elyse April
Illustrations by Lewis Agrell
This book celebrates healthy food, and encourages young children and their caregivers to eat well, and with greater awareness. (Ages: Infants-6)
ISBN: 978-1-890772-69-7, paper, 32 pages, $9.95
Spanish Language Version: *Nos Gusta Comer Bien*
ISBN: 978-1-890772-78-9

TO ORDER: 800-381-2700, or visit our website, www.hohmpress.com *Special discounts for bulk orders.